HarperCollins Children's Books, a division of HarperCollins Publishers,

10 East 53rd Street, New York, NY 10022.

www.harpercollinschildrens.com

Library of Congress Cataloging-in-Publication Data is available.

ISBN 978-0-06-196101-4

Typography by Joe Merkel

11 12 13 14 15   SCP   10 9 8 7 6 5 4 3 2 1

❖

First Edition

Hedgehug

a sharp lesson in love

created &
illustrated by
dan
pinto

written by
benn
sutton

HARPER
An Imprint of HarperCollinsPublishers

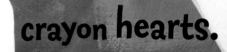

Hedgehug sat at his table drawing red crayon hearts.

Tomorrow was **Valentine's Day.**
The day he had been **waiting** and **waiting** for.

That night,
Hedgehug went to bed
as soon as the sun disappeared.

Tomorrow I'm going to
be in love, he thought.

In the morning, Hedgehug was awake **long** before his alarm clock rang.

He leaped from his bed, gripped his heart to his chest, and **burst**

UP and

out

of his

burrow.

The forest was **abuzz.**
Birds were singing, the
sun shone brightly, and
everything smelled **fresh**
and **exciting.** *Love is*
everywhere, thought
Hedgehug.

And then he saw her.

bathump-
bathump

"Hello, bunny." Hedgehug waved.
"I have something for you."

And he gave
the bunny his heart.

Hedgehug was
so happy he
could . . .

"OUCH!"

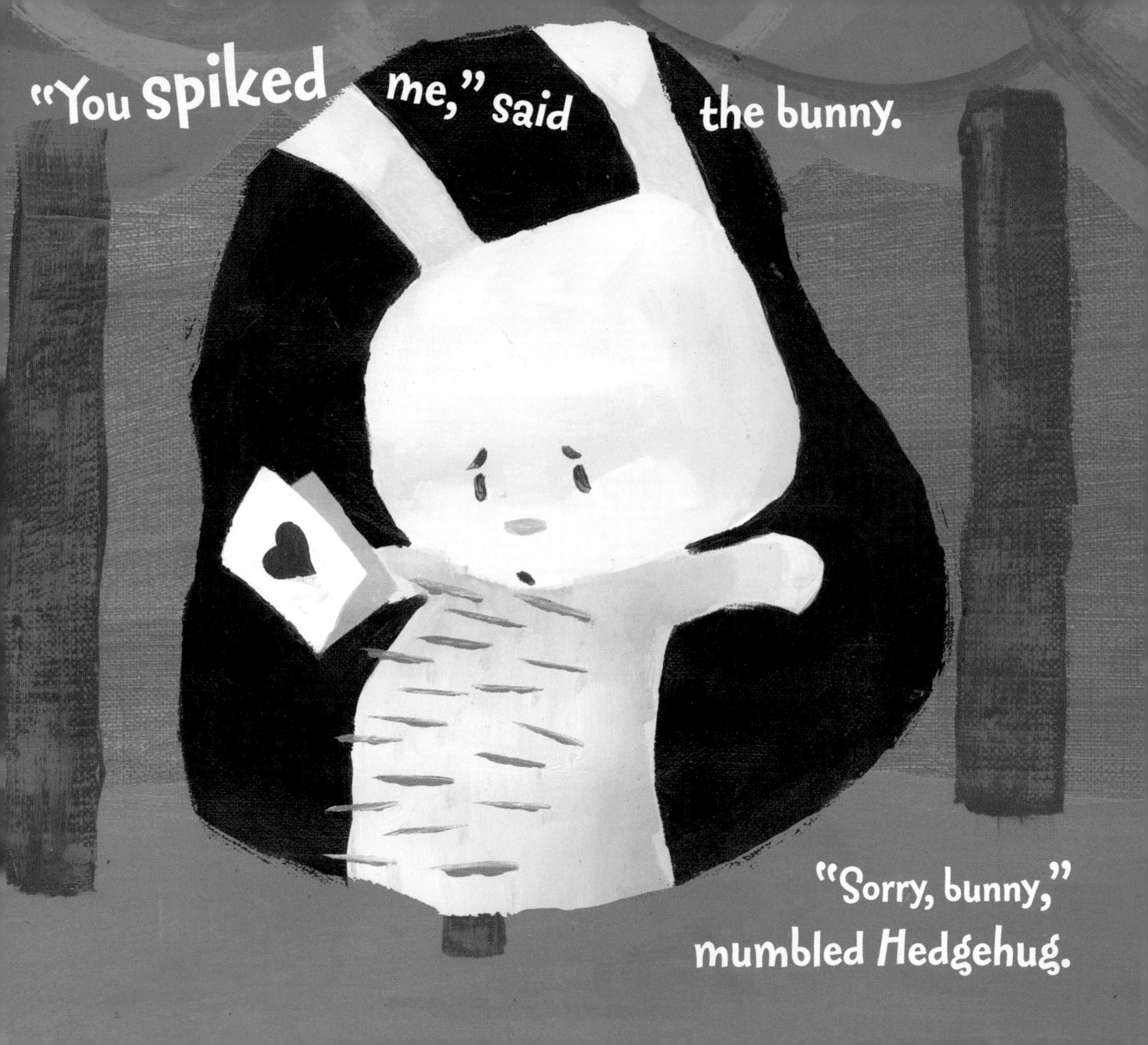

"You spiked me," said the bunny.

"Sorry, bunny," mumbled Hedgehug.

"My name isn't bunny, it's Doris! And I don't want your stupid heart!"

Doris stormed off.

Hedgehug picked up his heart
and was dusting it off when a
feather brushed his nose.

bathump-
bathump

There was only one thing
for Hedgehug to do.

"Hello, owl." Hedgehug smiled
when he reached the highest branch.

"I have **something** for you."
And he gave the owl his **heart**.

"My name isn't **owl**, it's Edie.
And I don't want your
silly heart.
Can't you see
I'm **sleeping?"**
growled
the owl.

The next thing Hedgehug knew,
he was flat on his stomach on the
floor of the forest . . .

. . . staring up at a boar.

"Hhh . . . hello," said Hedgehug.
"What's *your* name?"

Then Hedgehug   did something

he wished

he had not.

bathump-bathump,

bathump-bathump

went Hedgehug's heartbeat.

pathumpedy-pathumpedy,

pathumpedy-pathumpedy

went Hedgehug's feet.

THUMP!

went the boar.

Hedgehug picked up his **torn**,
crumpled heart from the forest floor.
But **this** time there was
nothing he could do
to fix it.

Love hurts.

Sore, tired, and alone,
Hedgehug headed for home.
He hadn't gone far when
there was a **tap** on his shoulder.

"Hello," said an armadillo. "I have something for you."

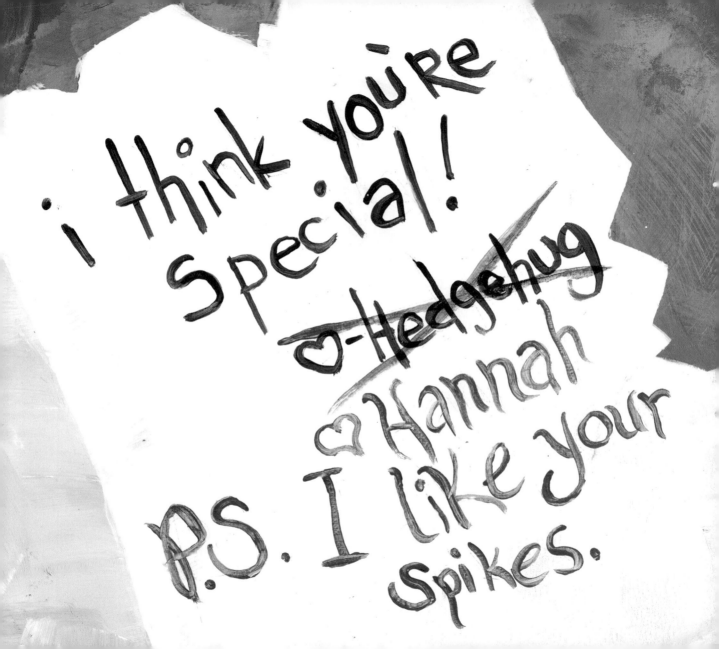

the end.

thanks to mom + dad, benn,
jeanmarie, mary-kate, and
everyone at harpercollins
(even suzan).
♡ - dan

thanks to dan,
jeanmarie, and the gorgeous
buddug.
♡ - benn